To my brother, Yoyo,

who took me to the ball game.

Atheneum Books for Young Readers

An imprint of Simon & Schuster Children's Publishing Division

1230 Avenue of the Americas

New York, New York 10020

Text copyright © 2006 by Sarah L. Thomson

Illustrations copyright © 2006 by Hanoch Piven

All rights reserved, including the right of

reproduction in whole or in part in any form.

Book design by Ann Bobco

The text for this book is set in Centaur MT.

The illustrations for this book are rendered in gouache and collages on paper.

Manufactured in the United States of America

First Edition

1 2 3 4 5 6 7 8 9 10

Library of Congress Cataloging-in-Publication Data

Piven, Hanoch, 1963–

What athletes are made of / Hanoch Piven

[illustrator ; text, Sarah L. Thomson].—1st ed.

p.   cm.

"Ginee Seo Books."

ISBN-13: 978-1-4169-1002-2

ISBN-10: 1-4169-1002-6

1. Athletes—United States—Caricatures and cartoons—Juvenile literature.

2. Athletes—United States—Biography—Juvenile literature.

I. Thomson, Sarah L. II. Title.

GV697 .A1P49 2006

796'.092'2—dc22   2005024841

SOURCES FOR QUOTATIONS

ALI: "Superman don't need no seat belt."
STEWARDESS: "Well, Superman don't need no airplane."
From: Crouser, Dick. "It's Unlucky to be Behind at the End of the Game" and Other Great Sports Retorts. New York: Quill, 1983.

ABDUL-JABBAR: "I would tell kids to pursue their basketball dreams, but I would tell them to not let that be their only dream. You should have dreams as students in addition to having dreams as athletes."
From: www.time.com/time/community/transcripts/1999/022599jabbar.html. (Accessed July 12, 2005)

RUTH: "I swing big, with everything I've got. I hit big or I miss big. I like to live as big as I can."
From: Herzog, Brad. The Sports 100: The One Hundred Most Important People in American Sports History. New York: Macmillian USA, 1985.

JOYNER-KERSEE'S COACH: "Do that again!"
From: Joyner-Kersee, Jacqueline, and Sonja Steptoe. A Kind of Grace: The Autobiography of the World's Greatest Female Athlete. New York: Warner Books, 1997.

GRETZKY'S FAN: "I can't believe you're the guy that scored all those goals!"
GRETZKY: "Sometimes I can't believe that either."
From: Grimsley, Will, and the Associated Press Staff. 101 Greatest Athletes of the Century. New York: Bonanza Books, distributed by Crown Publishers, 1987.

GRETZKY: "I couldn't beat people with my strength; I don't have a hard shot; I'm not the quickest skater in the league. My eyes and my mind have to do most of the work."
From: www.espn.go.com/sportscentury/features/00014218.html. (Accessed August 30, 2005)

SINGH (on Sorenstam): "She doesn't belong out here."
From: www.usatoday.com/sports/golf/pga/2003-05-12-sing_x.htm. (Accessed April 20, 2005)

HAMM: "[There's] no 'me' in Mia."; "The team, not the individual, is the ultimate champion. . . . I couldn't have scored one goal without my teammates."; "Secret weapon."
From: Hamm, Mia, and Aaron Heifetz. Go for the Goal: A Champion's Guide to Winning in Soccer and Life. New York: HarperCollins Publishers, 1999.

BECKHAM: "I don't care—I like it."
From: Daly, Steven. "Brand It Like Beckham." Vanity Fair, July 2004: 104–109, 146–150

WILLIAMS': "Welcome to the Williams show" (Mr. Williams's sign); "Family comes first, no matter how many times we play against each other."
From: Stout, Glenn. On the Court With . . . Venus and Serena Williams. Boston: Little, Brown, 2002.

GORDON'S MOTHER: "Slow down, slow down!"
GORDON: "Mom, the car won't go any slower."
From: Stout, Glenn. On the Track With . . . Jeff Gordon. Boston: Little, Brown, 2000.

POST-GAME RECAP PHOTOGRAPHIC CREDITS

All athlete photographs courtesy of the Associated Press.

What ATHLETES are made of

HANOCH PIVEN

ginee seo books

ATHENEUM BOOKS FOR YOUNG READERS   New York   London   Toronto   Sydney

Do you know how many home runs Babe Ruth hit in his career? Do you know how many soccer goals Mia Hamm scored in her first year with the U.S. National Team? Lots of people know scores and records about their favorite athletes. But sometimes we don't know as much about what great athletes are like as people.

This book will give you a glimpse into the lives of some of my favorite athletes. Most of them are admirable people. A few are not. Some are funny; some are serious; some are generous; some are modest; some are boastful. But they are all human, and they all love sports, just like I do—and probably you do too.

Even a great athlete who makes millions of dollars gets out onto the soccer field or the basketball court and competes just like any ordinary person who likes to kick a ball around or toss one through a hoop. Of course, some athletes are better than others, but the joy of being out there, doing your best, is the same for all of us.

I love that the world of sports is a world of truth. Whoever makes the better move, wins. When a player throws the ball, it either enters the basket or not. Reality cannot be twisted on the field.

There are many great athletes in the world, and I could not include all of them in this book. Instead I have selected athletes whose stories have a personal meaning for me. Some were chosen because of their undisputed greatness, and some because they have an inspiring or interesting story to tell.

I hope you enjoy discovering what these athletes are made of.

—Hanoch Piven

Three-time heavyweight champion **MUHAMMAD ALI** was known as much for boasting as he was for winning boxing matches. But he could also take a joke on himself. Once when he was on a plane, the flight attendant told him to fasten his seat belt. "Superman don't need no seat belt," he bragged. "Well, Superman don't need no airplane," she shot back. Ali fastened his seat belt.

rs at the end of each round. If a boxer is in trouble, the bell "saves" him—until the next round.

ATHLETES ARE MADE OF **GREAT MINDS**

KAREEM ABDUL-JABBAR

coached a high school basketball team on an Apache reservation. He told students to work hard in school as well as in sports. "I would tell kids to pursue their basketball dreams, but I would tell them to not let that be their only dream," he said. "You should have dreams as students in addition to having dreams as athletes."

DID YOU KNOW that Abdul-Jabbar was famous for his skyhook shot? With his back to the basket, he could hold the ball in one hand and launch it over his shoulder to score.

ATHLETES ARE MADE OF **FUNNY HABITS**

MICHAEL JORDAN's father, James, was good with machines (Michael wasn't). When James tinkered with a gadget, he had a habit of sticking out his tongue. Michael picked up this quirk and played basketball with his tongue out. After he became famous, thousands of kids learned to stick out their tongues just like Mike——and just like his father.

DID YOU KNOW that Jordan could dunk the ball by jumping from the free-throw line—more than thirteen feet away from the basket?

BABE RUTH

ate more, belched louder, and hit more home runs than anybody else—714 in his career. He made more money, too. In 1930 his salary was bigger than the president's. Ruth said, "I swing big, with everything I've got. I hit big or I miss big. I like to live as big as I can."

ATHLETES ARE MADE OF

A HUNGER FOR GREATNESS

DID YOU KNOW that one day in Coney Island (Brooklyn, New York), Babe Ruth drank eight sodas and ate four porterhouse steaks and eight hot dogs?

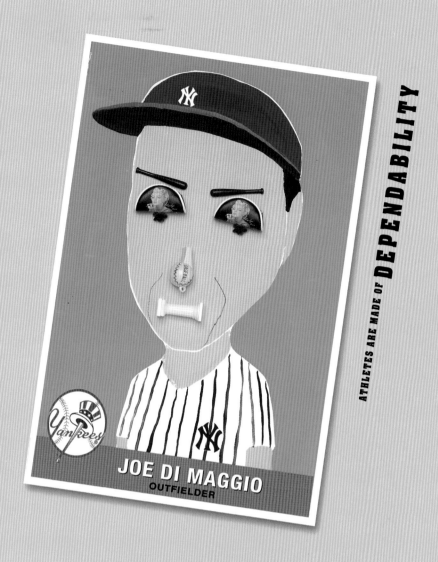

ATHLETES ARE MADE OF **DEPENDABILITY**

JOE DI MAGGIO
OUTFIELDER

In the summer of 1941, Americans were worried about World War II. But their spirits were lifted as JOE DiMAGGIO began to get at least one hit in game after game. How long could he keep it up? Even the cool DiMaggio was nervous, but that didn't affect his play. His streak lasted fifty-six games, a record that still stands more than sixty years later.

DID YOU KNOW that Joe DiMaggio married the actress Marilyn Monroe? They divorced, but after she died he sent roses to her grave every week for twenty years.

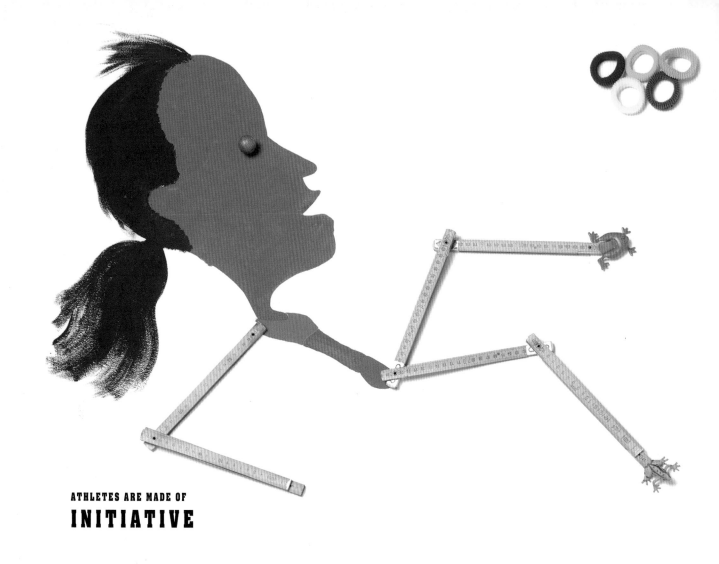

ATHLETES ARE MADE OF
INITIATIVE

As a kid, JACKIE JOYNER-KERSEE practiced the long jump at home, too shy to tell her coach that she wanted to try it. She brought sand back from the sandbox at the park to land in. When she did her first jump at the track, her coach yelled, "Do that again!" In the 1988 Olympics, Joyner-Kersee got a gold medal for the long jump and another for the heptathlon.

DID YOU KNOW that "hepta" means "seven" and "athlon" means "contest"? A heptathlon

During the 1936 Olympics in Berlin, Adolf Hitler was in power. He believed the Olympics would show that white, blond, blue-eyed people were smarter, stronger, and better than people of color. But black athletes like **JESSE OWENS** helped prove him wrong. Owens set two Olympic records and took home four gold medals.

ATHLETES ARE MADE OF **GET UP AND GO**

DID YOU KNOW that it was hard for Owens to make a living in the United States as a black track-and-field star? He even raced against horses for money.

BRAINS OVER BRAWN

Even though WAYNE GRETZKY is six feet tall, he doesn't look like a big guy next to other pro-hockey players. Once, at a hospital, a young fan exclaimed, "I can't believe you're the guy that scored all those goals!" Gretzky, nicknamed "The Great One," answered, "Sometimes I can't believe that either." He uses his intelligence rather than his size to win. He said, "I couldn't beat people with my strength; I don't have a hard shot; I'm not the quickest skater in the league. My eyes and my mind have to do most of the work."

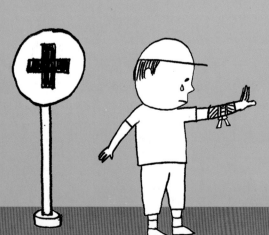

DID YOU KNOW that Gretzky liked to stand *behind* the goal and hit the puck from there? His passes wer

o perfect that sometimes the teammate who received the puck would just give it a tiny nudge to score.

A lot of great athletes start playing young—
but few as young as TIGER WOODS.
He was hitting golf balls with a miniature club before
he was a year old and got his first hole in one when he was six.
Fifteen years later Woods won the Masters Tournament at
twenty-one, the youngest person and the first African American to do so.

ATHLETES ARE
MADE OF
EARLY
STARTS

In 2003 ANNIKA SORENSTAM became the first woman in more than fifty years to play in a golf tournament against men. Some male players welcomed her; others didn't. "She doesn't belong out here," one said. But Sorenstam just tried to play her best. She didn't win, but she impressed everyone with her cool, calm style.

ATHLETES ARE MADE OF

TEAMWORK

MIA HAMM says there's "no 'me' in Mia." People have often called her the best female soccer player in the world, but to Mia it's more important to be part of a winning team. "The team, not the individual, is the ultimate champion," she says. "I couldn't have scored one goal without my teammates."

to his little sister? Mia was fast, tough, and smart. Their mom called her Garrett's "secret weapon."

ATHLETES ARE MADE OF

HANDY SKILLS

Many people think **DIEGO MARADONA** is the best soccer player ever, but sometimes he bent the rules. In a World Cup game against England he used his hand to score. Five minutes later he proved that he didn't need to cheat. He dribbled alone through five English players and made what is now called the best goal in World Cup history.

ATHLETES ARE MADE OF

SHOW-STOPPING GRACE

PELÉ may be the most popular athlete in the world. And he's probably the only sports figure who has stopped a war—or at least slowed one down. The two African nations of Biafra and Nigeria called off their war for two days, because Pelé was going to play in a soccer match that neither side wanted to miss.

DID YOU KNOW that the soccer team Diego Maradona played for as a kid won 136 matches in a row?

DID YOU KNOW that Pelé grew up so poor that he had to make his own soccer ball out of a sock stuffed with newspapers?

ATHLETES ARE MADE OF
FLASH AND DASH

A soccer player known for his spectacular goals and powerful kicks, **DAVID BECKHAM** makes headlines for wearing outrageous clothes. He liked to dress up when he was a kid, too. As the ring bearer in a wedding, he once wore knickerbockers, a frilly shirt, and ballet shoes. His father warned him that people might laugh, but David answered, "I don't care—I like it." He's still the same way today—he once wore pink nail polish to match his girlfriend's.

DID YOU KNOW that David Beckham's kick has been clocked at eighty miles per hour?

FOUR SPIRITS ARE MADE OF **FREE SPIRITS**

MARTINA
NAVRÁTILOVÁ

was born in Czechoslovakia at a time
when people there could not speak or
write freely or leave the country without permission.
At eighteen, Navrátilová came to America to play in the
U.S. Open and decided to stay here, even though it meant
being cut off from her family and friends. She went on to
win nine Wimbledon singles titles.

DID YOU KNOW that Navrátilová liked the food as well as the freedom of the United
States? She loved pancakes, pizza, ice cream, and hamburgers.

When **ANDRE AGASSI**'s tennis career began, he was a trendy teenager with a hip haircut and colorful shirts. Later, when his career was in trouble and he needed a fresh start, he shaved his whole body (including his head!), wore traditional white tennis clothes, and got up early to work out and practice. The effort paid off. He won a career grand slam, something only five other male players have ever done.

DID YOU KNOW that in tennis a grand slam means winning Wimbledor

he Australian Open, the U.S. Open, and the French Open tennis championships?

At the first Wimbledon tennis championship, two sisters played in the final match. More than a century later, it happened again. When **VENUS** and **SERENA WILLIAMS** faced off to decide the winner of the Lipton Championship, their father held up a sign: "Welcome to the Williams Show." The sisters play against each other often, but the competition doesn't keep them apart. "Family comes first, no matter how many times we play against each other," Venus said.

ATHLETES ARE MADE OF
CLOSE
COMPETITION

DID YOU KNOW that Serena Williams once played in the U.S. Open wearing boots and tha

Venus Williams has her own interior design business?

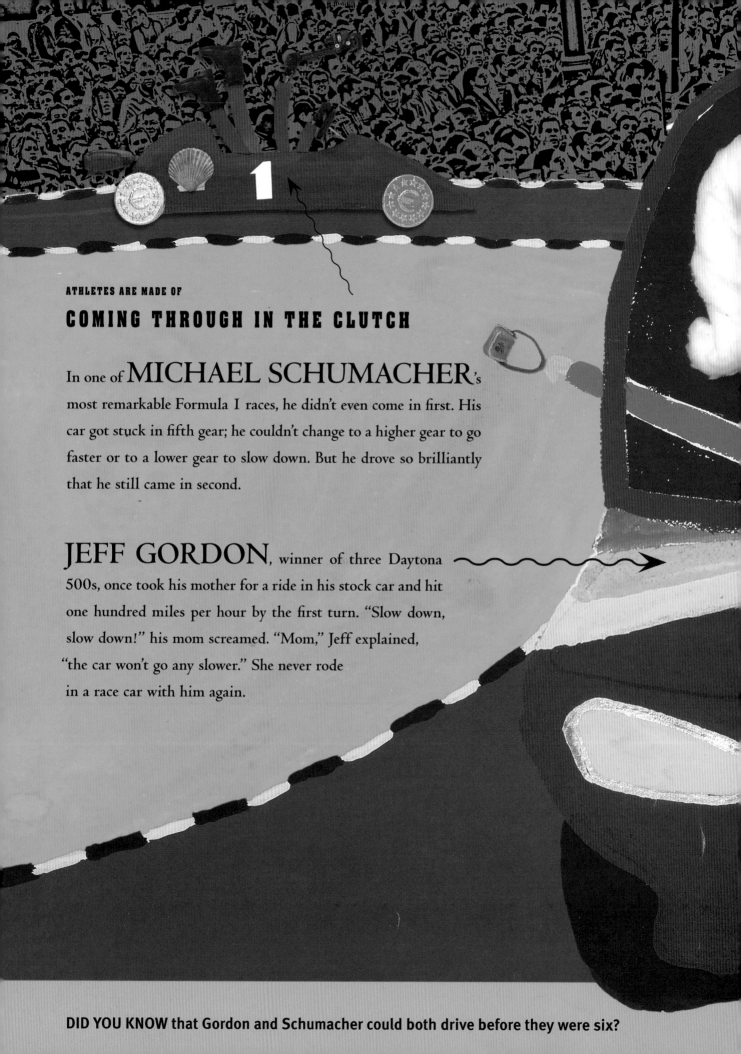

ATHLETES ARE MADE OF

COMING THROUGH IN THE CLUTCH

In one of MICHAEL SCHUMACHER's most remarkable Formula 1 races, he didn't even come in first. His car got stuck in fifth gear; he couldn't change to a higher gear to go faster or to a lower gear to slow down. But he drove so brilliantly that he still came in second.

JEFF GORDON, winner of three Daytona 500s, once took his mother for a ride in his stock car and hit one hundred miles per hour by the first turn. "Slow down, slow down!" his mom screamed. "Mom," Jeff explained, "the car won't go any slower." She never rode in a race car with him again.

DID YOU KNOW that Gordon and Schumacher could both drive before they were six?

ATHLETES ARE MADE OF **A NEED FOR SPEED**

Gordon drove a small car called a quarter midget by the age of five.
When Schumacher was four, he had a pedal kart with a motorcycle engine.

ATHLETES ARE MADE OF

TOUGH STUFF

JOE NAMATH hurt one knee in a college football game and damaged the other trying to favor the injured one. But he never let pain stop him. In one game Namath ended up playing with his usual bad knees plus a dislocated finger, a jammed thumb, a bad back, headaches, and dizziness. But he refused to quit and his team won.

DID YOU KNOW that Joe Namath was nicknamed "Broadway Joe" because he loved to stay

ATHLETES ARE MADE OF

LASTING LEGACIES

JIM THORPE not only won two gold medals in track and field at the 1912 Olympics—he also played football, baseball, basketball, lacrosse, tennis, golf, hockey, and more. Sadly, this remarkable athlete lost his Olympic medal because he had taken a small salary for playing baseball. (At that time anyone who had been paid money for a sport was not allowed in the Olympics.) Thorpe swore he didn't mean to break any rules. But his medals weren't returned until thirty years after he died.

DID YOU KNOW that Jim Thorpe was a Native American from the Sac-and-Fox tribe?

Once when **LANCE ARMSTRONG** was a teenager, he was struggling to finish a triathlon, a long race combining swimming, biking, and running. His mother was watching and told him not to quit, even if he had to walk to the finish line. That's just what he did. Later in his life, Armstrong got cancer. But he still didn't quit. After surgery and treatment, he returned and has won the Tour de France a record seven times. (Riders in this difficult race used to be allowed to take off their helmets.)

DID YOU KNOW that the leader of the Tour de France wears a special yellow jersey? The color was chosen

1919 because the newspaper that sponsored the race was printed on yellow paper.

POST-GAME RECAP: Statistics and career highlights

KAREEM ABDUL-JABBAR, b. 1947–
Scored a record 38,387 points in his career. • Named the NBA's Most Valuable Player six times. • Played for six NBA championship teams. • Led the NBA in scoring in 1970–1971 and 1971–1972. • Patented the skyhook shot.

ANDRE AGASSI, b. 1970– • Won a grand slam (Australian Open, French Open, Wimbledon, and U.S Open), something only five male players have ever done. • Won an Olympic gold medal in 1996. • Won sixty tournaments in his career. • Won the Australian Open four times.

MUHAMMAD ALI, b. 1942– • Won the light-heavyweight gold medal at the 1960 Olympics. • Defeated Sonny Liston in 1964 to become the heavyweight champion. • Defeated George Foreman in 1974 (in a match called "The Rumble in the Jungle," which was held in Zaire, Africa) to regain his heavyweight title. • Lit the Olympic flame in 1996.

LANCE ARMSTRONG, b. 1971– • Won the World Road Race Championship and was the U.S. National Championship in 1993. • Became the youngest rider (at twenty-one) to win a Tour de France stage. • Became the second American (after Greg LeMond) to win the Tour de France. • Won the Tour de France a record seven times in a row.

DAVID BECKHAM, b. 1975– • Made the "goal of the decade" in 1996, kicking the ball from the half-way line into the net to score. • Played on the Manchester United team that won the Premiership, the Football Association Cup, and the European Cup, the first time an English team won all three championships. • Scored 85 goals in 394 games for Manchester United.

JOE DiMAGGIO, b. 1914–d. 1999 • Set a hitting-streak record that still stands, getting at least one hit in fifty-six consecutive games. • Played in ten World Series and won nine. • Hit 361 home runs. • Achieved a lifetime batting average of .325. • Struck out only 369 times.

JEFF GORDON, b. 1971– • Won four Winston Cup titles. • Won three Daytona 500s. • Became the youngest driver (at twenty-four) to win the Winston Cup and the youngest (at twenty-five) to win the Daytona 500. • Named Rookie of the Year in cup racing in 199

WAYNE GRETZKY, b. 1961– • Scored 2,85 points and 884 goals. • Made 1,963 assists. • Set a record for most goals in a season (ninety-two). • Won the Ha trophy (for most valuable player) nine times and the Ro trophy (for scoring) ten times.

MIA HAMM, b. 1972– • Became the world's all-tim leading scorer, male or female, in international competitio with 158 goals. • Played on two winning Women's Worl Cup teams. • Won two Olympic gold medals. • Name player of the year in 2000 and 2001 by FIFA (Fédéracio Internationale de Football Association). • Was the young est player (at fifteen) to compete for the U.S. women national soccer team. • Was the youngest player (at nin teen) on the Olympic team.

MICHAEL JORDAN, b. 1963– • Scored 32,29 points in his career, the fourth-highest scorer in th NBA. • Led the NBA in scoring a record ten times. Scored more than three thousand points in a single se son, the second player (besides Wilt Chamberlain) to d so. • Named the NBA's Most Valuable Player five time

JACKIE JOYNER-KERSEE, b. 1962– • Won s Olympic medals (three gold, one silver, two bronze), mo than any other female athlete in track and field. • Set world record by scoring 7,291 points in the heptathlon, seven-event competition. Set an Olympic record in the lo jump. • Was unbeaten in track-and-field competition b any other American for thirteen years.

DIEGO MARADONA, b. 1960– • Scored "th goal of the century" in the 1986 World Cup match betwee Argentina and England. • Was captain and Most Valu able Player when Argentina won the World Cup in 1986. Played in three World Cup finals. • Began playing in inte national competition at sixteen.

JOE NAMATH, b. 1943– • Quarterbacked an upset Super Bowl win for the New York Jets against the favored Baltimore Colts. The Jets were the first AFL team to win the Super Bowl. • Became the only quarterback to pass for four thousand yards in a fourteen-game season. • Named the AFL's Most Valuable Player in 1968.

MARTINA NAVRÁTILOVÁ, b. 1956– • Won a record nine Wimbledon titles, including six in a row. • Won four U.S. Opens, three French Opens, and two Australian Opens. • Won 167 singles titles, more than any other tennis player. • Won seventy-four matches in a row, the current women's record.

JESSE OWENS, b. 1913–d. 1980 • Set three world records and tied one more at a single track-and-field match in 1935, including a world record in the long jump that stood for twenty years. • Won four gold medals in the 1936 Olympics in Berlin. • Voted the greatest track-and-field star for the first half of the twentieth century in an Associated Press poll. • Received the Medal of Freedom in 1976.

PELÉ, b. 1940 – • Scored 1,283 goals in his career. • Played on Brazil's winning 1958 World Cup team at seventeen and made two goals in the final match. • Was the first soccer player to play on three winning World Cup teams.

BABE RUTH, b. 1895–d. 1948 • Hit 714 home runs in his career, a record undefeated until 1974. • Led the American League in home runs for twelve seasons. • Was the first to hit sixty home runs in a season. • Achieved a .342 batting average. • Helped lead the Yankees to their first four World Series. • Played for the 1927 Yankees team, often called the best in history.

MICHAEL SCHUMACHER, b. 1969 – Won a record seven Formula I championships. • Won thirteen out of eighteen races in 2004. • Became the youngest driver to win consecutive Formula I World Championships in 1994–95.

ANNIKA SORENSTAM, b. 1970– • Won sixty-two LPGA tournaments. • Shot the lowest-scoring round (fifty-nine) in LPGA history. • Named Rolex Player of the Year seven times. • Won Sweden's Athlete of the Year Award.

JIM THORPE, b. 1888–d. 1953 • Won an Olympic gold medal in pentathlon in 1912. • Won an Olympic gold medal and set a world record score of 8,412 points in the decathlon in 1912. • Named the first president of the American National Football Association (which became the NFL).

SERENA WILLIAMS, b. 1981– • Named "Most Impressive Newcomer of the Year" by the WTA in 1998. • Achieved a grand slam. This was labeled a "Serena Slam" because she held all four championships at the same time. • Entered her first tournament at five and a half. • Won the gold medal in doubles tennis at the 2000 Olympics. • Won both the singles and doubles championships at the Australian Open in 2003.

VENUS WILLIAMS, b. 1980– • Named "Most Impressive Newcomer of the Year" by the WTA in 1997. • Became the first African American to reach the number one ranking on the WTA tour. • Named "Sports Woman of the Year" in 2000 by *Sports Illustrated for Women*. • Won an Olympic gold medal in singles and doubles in 2000. • Hit the fastest serve in WTA history (127.4 miles per hour). • Was the Wimbledon champion in singles and doubles in 2000.

TIGER WOODS, b. 1975– • Became the youngest golfer (at twenty-one) and the first African American to win the Masters Tournament. • Became the youngest golfer (at twenty-four) to win a grand slam (winning the Masters Tournament, the U.S. Open, the British Open, and the PGA Championship). • Won the U.S. Open in 2000 at twelve under par, winning by fifteen shots. • Won the British Open in 2000 with nineteen under par.